Songs of the Mearns

Rodger Lyall

To Terry

For her abiding patience and support without which none of this would have been possible

Chapter 1

Lewis Grassic Gibbon Inspiration

Lewis Grassic Gibbon was the pen name of **James Leslie Mitchell,** born in Aberdeenshire in 1901 but raised in Arbuthnott and schooled at nearby Stonehaven. Mitchell wrote numerous books and shorter works under both his real name and his Pen name before his early death in 1935. It was his trilogy entitled 'A Scots Quair' with which he made his mark.

Songs in this chapter

Chris
The Pig and its Mistress
Circin's Song
Garvock's Ghaist
The Path of Man
Guthrie's Royal Toun
Pillars of Cloud

Chris

In the closing paragraphs of Grey Granite, Chris Guthrie returns to her roots in Echt and climbs the Barmekin. Gibbon says, 'She sat on as one by one the lights went out and the rain came, beating the stones about her, and falling all that night while she sat there, presently feeling no longer the touch of rain or hearing the sound of lapwings going by.' Her fate is left for the reader to conclude. It is a beautifully descriptive passage and called out for a song to be written.

Chris

The peesies fly ower Barmekin
Returning here is strange
Thistles grown around Cairndhu
Nothing's left but change and change

Change of season, change of being
The lad I lo'e lies at the Somme
Only now the land enduring
The peesies wail to call me home

Step by step I clutch the heather
Flowing like a sea of wine
Bennachie and Fare lie sleeping
'Gold, then red, as up I climb

Last road found and gladly taken
Concerning none and none concerned
Looking far across the sky
The day goes east to never die

Bennachie walks to the night
Farmhouse lights hold one last glow
The rain is softly falling now
And Chris, once fine, is here no more

The Pig and its Mistress

In 'Cloud Howe,' Lewis Grassic Gibbon tells the story which I composed in this song, after giving a brief introduction as follows: 'the foul brute would go home, near every night as drunk as a toff, and fall into bed by the side of his wife, she'd say 'you course brute, you've come drunken again' but he'd only groan, with his hand at his stomach, the worm on the wriggle like a damned sea-serpent.'

The Pig and Its Mistress

It was Armistice Eve when Jim the Stourock
Fell into the bed by the side of his wife
Drunk as the pig which he kept in the sty
Ready for Dite tae kill bye and bye
    Repeat Chorus,: Pig on the loose, wife in the hoose
Jim on the booze, Dite makin' news

The next day Dite took his axe tae the beast
The beastie began tae scraich and screech
He grinned at the pig and then at the wife
Syne took a dram and then his knife

The mistress took leave her sister tae bide
Dite was for killin' the beastie alive
Took a run at the pig in the dimly lit barn
Swung the axe and collapsed in the sharn

A puckle hoors later the beastie wis hingin'
Just aboot finished stringin' and drippin'
Dite an idea, the secret he kept
Of a pig in the bed where the Stourock's wife slept

An hour or so later, the Stourock cam home
His drunken heid spinnin, a ship in a storm
Unsnecked the door and loosened his beets
Shoggled tae bed and joggled the beast

He said mistress Jean, ye feel afae cauld
Then scraiched oot, a demented soul
A friend pointed to the pig and its spillage
The Stourock said man, it fair looked her image

Circin's Song

The Circins were a Pictish clan who occupied the territory of Kincardineshire or what is now unimaginatively named South Aberdeenshire by the bureaucrats. Their leader was King Gric who founded a church at St. Cyrus, otherwise well regarded for its pristine sands.

Gibbon was a diffusionist who believed that man became civilised at the cost of his personal freedom – as opposed to man's nomadic ancestors who roamed the world unencumbered by possessions and class structures, without religion or hierarchy. This was, for Gibbon, man's golden age and placed in the context of when he lived, during the depression years, this is perhaps all the more understandable. I loved this perhaps romantic view of life, particularly when set alongside the harsh reality of farming in the Mearns. It was this that inspired me to write and record so many songs and poems

Circin's Song

I am the nomad of the Mounth
The hunter by the morning star
The fisher by the Circin sands
The gatherer of roots by hand
My song is carried on the wind
As up the War-Woof Cairn we climb
You hear me in the wind that soochs
You see me in the frosty rime

On Circin sands, the wildfowl winter
The fallow deer's my fellow sprinter
In fields now ploughed, my axe still glints
My prey brought down by bone and flint
We hunt and fish as brothers all
No one of us allowed to fall
We touch the warmth of sun-stained clay
The stars above us map our way

And high in the race of wind and time
We naked roam the peaks we climb
Mating as the beasts and birds
From the stone ring comes our sacred word
On sunlit slopes we cast our breath
With simpleness we meet our death
In the Long Cairn now my chieftain sleeps
As the sun grows still on the far Mounth peak

Back to first verse

Garvock's Ghaist

Grassic Gibbon told this tale in 'Cloud Howe.' I adapted it for the song and narrative on my CD, 'A Tale of the Howe.' The song was a winning entry in the national Burnsong contest in 2007. Here is the background.

'Oot o' the Royal toun and ye're intae the Garvock and thereby stands a tale. It was there that David De Berkeley, laird o' Maithers, wi Lauriston, Arbuthnott, Pitarrow and Hakerton slaughtered John Melvillle o' Glenbervie.

Weel, it seems Melville's neighbours had suffered enough and complained tae Jamie Stuart doon in Edinburgh. Jamie was right vexed and he pulled at his beard and said – "Sorrow gin the Sheriff were sodden, - sodden and supped in his brew" and man, they took him at his word and invited Melville tae hunt in the forest o' the Garvock. Then they kindled a fire, boiled a muckle cauldron o' water between two stones, seized the sheriff, stripped him naked and threw him intae the boiling water. Aifter that, each of them took their horn spoons from their belts, supped frae the ghastly brew and fulfilled the words that the king had said. It seems the sheriff howled like a wolf in the warming water, then like a bairn smored in plague, slowly ceased tae scraich, his body reid as the Mearns clay, till the flesh loosed aff his seething bones. King Jamie, aye him that was sitting doon in Edinburgh, pronounced the lairds outlaws and vowed that Berkley would never be given peace tae live either on land or sea. So damn the bit,did Berkley no go and build a bit kaim on a cliff top eyrie at the Milton o' Mathers.'

Garvocks's Ghaist

As I blew in by Garvockside
And by yon Broonieleys man
I saw a kettle brewin' fast
Wi' the sheriff boilin' raw man
The noble lairds they danced aroond
The sheriff scraiched and howled man
They supped the brew, they supped the brew
And slavered on the thocht man

I whipped around the bonny fire
And fanned the embers braw man
Till Berkley shouted tae his freend
Arbuthnott, what a draw man
If Jamie had been here the day
A happier king he'd be man
Tae see yon Melville o'er and dane
Upon oor Garvock hill man

He wis sae prood and aye did strut
He glowered yon orra e'e man
We had tae bring him doon a bit
And that's the end o' that man
When I am in my Mather's Kaim
Between the land and sea man
I will be safe from Jamie's wrath
I will'na lose nae sleep man

When Jamie Stuart heard o' this
He minded on his words man
Gin he were sodden and supped in bree
He wisnae tae dee like yon man
These Mearns' lairds will pay the price
They'll hae nae peace at a' man
They'll no be safe by land or sea

I'll hae them pay the price man

Arbuthnott, Mathers and Pittarow
Wi Lauriston and Graeme man
Were helpit by their freends in court
The thing wis pit tae rest man
A chapel was built in auld Drumskite
Daily prayers were said man
For Melville's soul, boiled in the pot
At the top o' the Garvock hill man

The Path Of Man

'The Path of Man' was my first attempt at songwriting and was inspired by the minister's sermon in 'Sunset Song.' Lewis Grassic Gibbon narrated 'So hardly a soul paid heed to his reading, except Chris and her father, she thought it fine; for he told of the long dead beasts of the Scottish land in the times when jungle flowered its forests across the Howe and a red sun rose on the steaming earth that the feet of man had still to tread: and he pictured the dark, slow tribes that came drifting across the low lands of the northen seas, the great bear watched them come, and they hunted and fished and loved and died, God's children in the morn of time; and he brought the first voyagers sailing the sounding coasts, they brought the heathen idols of the great Stone Ring, the Golden Age was over and past and lust and cruelty trod the world.'

The Path Of Man

Ae morn lang syne, I dandered doon
The sleeping Gaerlie granite mounds
Through jungled forests in the Howe
And plains that hadnae seen a plough
The steaming earth was sun-parched red
The feet o' man had still to tread
I found my way past rock and tree
And river fit mair did ye see?

The years went by, the wild bear watched
As tribes of men the Great stane stood
They hunted, fished and looe'd and died
They cleared the land and changed its mood
Wi' weapons, coins and tools of flint
They forward moved fae in ahent
And tell me as your path it ran
Fit happened tae the life o' man

Italian men in columns drove
And sa' the good folk o' the Mearns
Who served as tenants in their swamps
Tae maisters new, a gentry breed
They sweated through a lifetime's chore
Of clearing whins and stane and bog
Aye this was how things changed fir man
But more I sa' as on I ran

Doonstream, I cam upon a plain
That had been passed by power of man
To local lairds, the land they froze
And oot of this a village rose
Friars of the Carmelite
Had bigged their midden on a hill
And man gave up the freedom past
To build the structures o' this class

And then much later in my time
While flowing in full river spate

The north sea thundered through a mist
My run could feel the hand of fate
A course cauld wind sooched through the whins
The new toon people glowered in fear
A king had landed on their beach
Tae refuge tak, well oot o' reach

They welcomed him and cared a bit
He favoured them as he sa' fit
Wi' new found powers to work and trade
Flax spinning mills, fine sail cloth made
A sailing ship to beat the rest
Farming land, by far the best
But noo I speir fae my time span
Fit wis the better life for man?

Guthrie's Royal Toun

During 2003, I decided to collect some songs from my home county of Kincardineshire but failed. There simply weren't many. So I started writing them myself. That led to the creation of a variety of own material, one of which received a winning award in the national Burnsong contest of 2007.

This particular song was written about my home town of Bervie, of which Lewis Grassic Gibbon wrote 'There are two things especially noticeable about Bervie; the unlimited confidence of the inhabitants in their own ability; and secondly their pride in being townspeople of a Royal Burgh. How it became a royal burgh there is no accurate account; although most of the 'citizens' have a vague notion that it was through a certan King David (but which King David, no one even professes to guess).'

Well this was the story that I was told as a boy.

Guthrie's Royal Toun

Shipwreck in the Bervie bay, Dave the Bruce has come tae stay
Followed by the coats of red, he takes a leap and onward sped
Wi' his quine past chapel well, he met a fisherman
Feed me from your catch of fish and you'll enjoy a richer dish

Wife o' wife pit on the fire, help the King and mak him drier
Grease the pan and heat the stove, knead the dough and mak a loaf
I'll gut twa herrin for the King, no you'll nae dae sic a thing
Gut three herrin fisherwife to bring the mannie back tae life

Full o' smeddum Davy said, kneel doon man and bow your head
From this day on the toun is free and your own name will be Gut Three
The land doon in the haughs you get, fae this day on wi' oot a let
And for the folks wha live aroond, this place will be a Royal Toon

No scholar's studies o' the books could find this story or its source
But folks aroond the toun still say, Guthrie's dam is fished the day
For finnocks and for other fish that help tae pay the bills
As Davy watches fae his crag, the royal toun's new spinning mills

Pillars of Cloud

A song inspired from the words of Chris in Lewis Grassic Gibbon's 'Cloud Howe.'
'And she thought then, looking on the shadowed Howe with its stratus mists and pillars of spume, driving west by the Leachie bents, that men had followed these pillars of cloud like men lost in the high, dreich hills, they followed and fought and toiled in the wake of each whirling pillar that rose from the heights, clouds by day to darken men's minds - loyalty and fealty, patriotism, love, the mumbling chants of the dead old gods that once were worshipped in the circles of stones, christianity, socialism, nationalism – all - Clouds that swept through the Howe of the world, with men that took them for gods; just clouds, they passed and finished, dissolved and were done, nothing endured but the Seeker himself, him and the everlasting Hills.'

Pillars of Cloud

Stratus cloud ships sailed the morn
As Trusta slept at the edge of dawn
Wandering tribes crossed the Doggar bank
To carve a place where fortune shone
They built pillars of rock towards the sun
As clouds gathered round the work they'd begun
They built pillars of faith, religion and stone
Like clouds, these have vanished, dissolved and are gone

Chorus: Cloud pillars by day
Fire pillars by night
Old dreams now seen as a fantasy flight
New clouds soon gather
Then drift and are gone
Like the dew comes at night
And is gone in the morn

Cirrus cloud ships welcomed spring
Peewits flew high above clear water streams
Young folk came calling, through bracken and fern
Gathered together to build brave new dreams
They found pillars of cloud, their hopes to abate
Pillars of Nationhood, Church and the State
Pillars of cloud, formed not for endurance
Only the land could give that assurance

Nimbus cloud ships sailed the dawn
A sunrise unending from far in the east
The auld stanes stood ringed, their dreams long put past
Creeds and beliefs now forever outcast
With pillars of State and Religion away
The folk of the land gazed to find a new way
Between cloud and land, brave hopes now allowed
No longer imprisoned by pillars of cloud

Chapter 2

Other Songs From The Mearns

I was brought up in Inverbervie, three miles from where Lewis Grassic Gibbon lived in the early years of his life. Having read his work, I realised I identified strongly with much of what he had written. The following are a few songs I decided to write from my own personal viewpoint.

Songs:

The Auld Brig
The Field of Flowers
Moving On
The Renegade Fishers
The Black Haired Gypsy Lass

The Auld Brig

During my younger years, I used to wander along the old bridge that spanned the river Bervie. I pondered on the changes the bridge must have seen over the centuries and that brought the inspiration to write a song. Below the old bridge were the remnants of a much earlier version and above it, towered its replacement built in the 1930s to camouflage the structure and distract the German bombers of WW2. This song goes back much further and provides some of my imagined thoughts of the activities that must have taken place around the old bridge and the people who passed alongside it over the ages.

The Auld Brig

From where I stand abin the flow
It's easy come and easy go
No fine start and no fine end
Eternity round every bend
Gin man thinks he controls his fate
It's forrit I just watch and wait
For they all pass like the leaves ablow
Nane o' them outlast the flow.

In days gone by, the hunters came
And roamed the peaks and haughs below
Free and swift on sunlit slopes
No challenges, no dreams, no hopes
With coloured skins, they raced the wind
Then by and by there came a change
But they all pass like the leaves below
Nane o them outlast the flow

Change to a faster tempo

My name is King Gric o' the Viri Na Moerne
I've been in this land since the day it was born
As I look all around, no challenge I see
The Romans pit doon and my people are free
We've fought the foe off, like nae ither's done
Protected our folk frae the cruel rule o' Rome
We're ready and able for challenges new
But there's little time left and we've so much to do

I am Davy Bruce, I've landed here too
I rule a' the lands tae the far distant North
I've gien you powers to work and to trade
And there's nae doubtin that you've been handsomely paid
I'll gie you a charter afore the sun's doon

And then I'm awa tae auld Reekie toon
Show that yer good folk, be honest and true
I'd like tae help mair but I've so much to do

Tae Dunnottar I've journeyed, I am Rabbie Burns
To see what is left of its fortress remains
My grandfather toiled here, the gardens tae till
Wis syne forced tae lease on at auld Clochanhill
We're living in Ayr noo, in land that is fair
The Howe wis ower haird, the land was left bare
And I've lairned tae dae mair than maister the ploo
I've penned Scotia's songs and I've much mair to do

I'm Hercules Linton, I've built a fine ship
She's a clipper and fast as the wind on the peaks
From the far eastern ocean tae the wild North sea
There's no a ship slicker or faster than she
Her name's Cutty Sark, just watch how she turns
She's fair a fine tribute tae auld Rabbie Burns
I made her the pride o' her captain and crew
But there wisnae much time gien for what I'd to do

I'm a chiel that's cried Mitchel, a writer to trade
I've studied the land o' the Mearns and its parks
Frae the cup o'the Howe, tae the poverty traps
I've much mair tae write, gin my mind will bide sharp
It's said I'm a chiel wi a mind o' my ain
Naething tae prove tae the folks o' my hame
My words are of land, the sun and the dew
But I'd little time left and I'd so much to do

We're the men o'the North, we're strong and we're hard
We've been tae the far waars, oor kinfolk tae guard
We're maistered the rigs on land and at sea
We've aywyes been ready tae work for a fee
Oor line gaes richt back tae the Viri Na Moerne

Richt back tae the days afore Scotia was born
We're sure fitted and proud o' aathing we do
And we've plenty time left, dae ye nae think that's true?

The Field Of Flowers
(English translation for Auchenblae)

My family originated, at least during the early 18th century, from Auchenblae in the Mearns. They were farmers who introduced the potato crop to the County. However, it was one of their sons who attracted the greatest attention. As a ship's surgeon and botanist, he was one of a crew to sail the first vessel in history to break through the Antarctic polar ice. His name was David Lyall and he is associated with the naming of over 2000 Antarctic plants that are recorded at Kew gardens.

The Field Of Flowers

From the field of flowers at Auchenblae
By Aberdeen, he made his way
Bound for the Moari Arctic shores
To a barren land, yet unexplored

The Terror and the Acheron
Left, far behind, the polar dawn
Now plashing through the spume and hail
Past ice clad cliffs in billowed sail

First men to breach the hard pack Ice
No thoughts of human sacrifice
And as they watched the albatross
Lyall found the white Ranunculus

And as he further walked and climbed
He found new species all around
A sea of white beyond his gaze
Part of a multi coloured blaze

Then late In eighteen fifty two
The loss of Franklin and his crew
Caused Lyall to search the North ice flow
Where lilies flower and whale fish blow

His fruitless journey round the Pole
Had undermined his desperate goal
And trundling through the rock and snow
He saw new crops of flowers grow

Westminster notes Lord
Franklin's fame
While Orkney shares a different name
And Kew displays more quietly
The Arctic flowering Lyalliii

At London Road in Cheltenham town,
Where Lyall lived and settled down
A plaque in England's leafy bowers
Makes tribute to the Field of Flowers

Moving On.

'Moving On' was written following a challenge to the members of the Grassic Gibbon Songwriters to write a song of that name. It inspired me to create some words about my home town and how I was forced to move on from where I had lived and what the Burgh had been.

Moving On

Leave the mill town by the river
Throw its old ways to the breeze
New found wealth drilled underground
Fortunes from the icy seas

Never heed the flax and fishing
Remnants from a bygone day
Move on, move on from the past
Change is what is here to stay

Leave your family by the fireside
Leave its values for today
A new world now will take its place
Change on change is underway

Never heed the fireside evenings
A different way, a better way
Move on, move on to the new world
Change to now, it's here to stay

Move on, move on, life soon passing
Dimming thoughts of bygone days
Old ways gone and near forgotten
Change has been the price to pay

But
Remember now the flax and fishing
Remember now old family ways
Most have gone, yet still remembered
Change can wait another day

The Renegade Fishers

It was around the year 2006 when the inhabitants of Inverbervie were notified that the ancient Royal Burgh Charter awarded to them by King David 11 was to be changed, such that their rights to fish the river Bervie freely, were going to be recinded. The town was in uproar and I wrote a song.

The Renegade Fishers

Oor Rab The Bruce faced Lanky Shank

Tae mak us independent

Then sired a son, aye Dave the same

Tae tak aheed the royal name

Noo Davy wis a cannier chiel

Wha likeit Royal Toons

And grantin toon folk fishin rights

Tae sport in ony wye they liked

Chorus

Gied fishin rights tae snigger troot

Stopped ithers comin in aboot

Gied Burgh rights tae local folk

The Common Good's noo just a joke

But now an act of treachery

By Deeside Salmon Fishery

Brings plans tae bring the Stoney whip

Tae stop the Bervie fishin rip

But they didna reckon Ashie Reid

Like Brucie independent

Sayin local folk will manage fine

Oor charters no recinded

Chorus

Gied fishin rights tae snigger troot

Stopped ithers comin in aboot

Gied Burgh rights tae local folk

The Common Good noo just a joke

The Black Haired Gypsy Lass

An entirely fictional tale about a young farming lad who travels to Bervie to visit many well-known local haunts along the way, before meeting, falling in love and settling down with a gypsy lass from up the coast at Catterline.

The Black Haired Gypsy Lass

As I cam in the Cowgate
And by the Mairket Square
My cairt filled up wi winter grain
And ither fairming fare
I was a stranger tae the toon
And sat doon for a dram
Wi a fairmer chiel and merchant loon
Tae hear the local yarn

The day rolled on
The nichtime came
And mony a tale wis telt
O' kings and crowns and scepters
And loyalty unsell't
As by and by, the flames grew low
The landlord snecked the door
So I spiered for my directions
Along the rocky shore

At crack o' day, I made my way
Alang the Fishergate
And doon the Kirkyburn syne went
The riverside to wait
At the icebox and the saltings
I watched the fisher folk
Then took the ford across the burn
Syne climbed the winding slope

Just as the sun rose in the sky
A fairmer cried 'fine day'
This road will tak ye tae Steenhive
Alang the clifftop way
Ye'll see King Davie's Chapel Well
Wi Merks strewn roond its tracks
But mind the track it narras
Roond Kinghornie's crossit stacks

Doon by the shore, beside the caves
A fisher mends his creels
Said from his boat you'd easy see
A broch amang the fields
But when ashore as try you might

Tae find that ancient site
You might as well catch lobsters
Wi fishin nets at night

And then he telt anither tale
Aboot a country wife
Who rescued Scotland's treasures
Frae Cromwell's reign o' strife
As doon the cliffs the sea it girned
And grumbled at the rocks
She brocht them frae Dunnottar
Hid well beneath her frocks

Then, as I cam by Catterline
The gloamin fair shone fine
I met a black-haired gypsy lass
Casting her fishing line
We yarned a while, we grew fell close
She shot a knowing glance
I kent I had tae tak the reins
And leave it then tae chance

We wandered back alang the coast
This gypsy quine and me
We laid oorsels aside the broch
Slept roch aside the sea
Next day aside the Chapel Well
Just by the fields of flax
I asked if she would bide wi' me
Blessed at the crossit stacks

So, whiles we bide at Fishergate
And hear the rushing stanes
And whiles we bide at Catterline
As the bloom comes on the whins
And in atween they places
Is where oor twa hairts are
Tae touch the raging sea at nicht
Then thank the morning star

The Bervie Alamo
(A nonsense song)

He strolled intae the Sally Bar
Ae cauld and rainy nicht
His hands a cut and chappit
He looked an orra sicht
His breeks were hingin doon his erse
His face wis full o' plukes
The barman asked him fa he wis
Wis he a heillan teuch?

He said I am a Bervie loon
Nae country lad or pleuchter
I work doon at the Linty mill
This loon's nae heillan teuchter
Pit up yer dukes ye Gurdon chiel
If this is hoo yer feelin
Fae this day on me and ma pals
Are drinkin' at the Creel Inn

At this the barman louped the bar
An' scattered a' the halfs
The spinners in the bar turned round
A bunch o' Dundee nyaffs
Haud on ye Gurdon fisherman
And dinna be a scunner
At this, the door swung open wide
In cam three hards fae Johnner

I'll need some help fae Gurdon noo
So please send reinforcements
But it was said the Sally chiel
Was needin' three and fourpence
An so a battle then broke out
Wi chips and mealies fleein'
Wi Bannerman's pies and Richie's fries
And kippers on the ceilin'

The bar door swung ajar again
The Gurdon lads were near
They formed a forrit airmy line
The doupers took the rear
The Bervie loons cowered roond the room
And by the one-armed bandit
The meenister ca'd the elders up
Then tannoyed from his pulpit

Cam all ye teuchters fae the North
You pleuchters on the broo
If we're tae save auld Bervie toon
We'll need a bloodless coo
At this the pleuchters lookit queer
Wantin' nae hand in a coo
When just at that, the Bervie loon
Opened up his moo

He said this things gone far aneuch

We'll hae nae fecht the necht
We dinna want nae heillan teuchs
Tellin us fit's wrang and richt
We Bervie, Gurdon, Jonner lads
We will nae langer spat
And man tae man the hale coast doon
Will brithers be (and a' that)

They sing this sang richt doon the coast
Wi muckle hairt and sole
Frae Catterline tae the Rio Tay
And occasionally, the Warehole
Across the 90 highway
Intae the land o' pleuchters
And even far intae the north
Amang the heillan teuchters

He said I am a Bervie loon
Nae country lad or pleuchter
I work doon at the Linty mill
This loon's nae heillan teuchter
At this, the hale bar gathered round
And offered up a cheer
And that is why these freendships last
Intae the present year

Chorus
Saddle up high
Stirrups doon low
Ride up the braes
In yer cooboy clathes
For the Bervie Alamo

Feels Like Coming Home

A challenge set to the Grassic Gibbon Songwriter's Group to describe what they felt about songwriting. This was my contribution. Fortunately, it is a song of the past. Not the best piece of work I fear and perhaps worth working on, a little more.

Feels Like Coming Home
I've tried to find a way, to lead this life of mine
I've been trying hard to catch dreams, all the time
I've been up and down the path of hope, often on my own
Now song writing feels like coming home

It's hard to travel on your own
Chasing fortunes round every stone
But when I get the urge to roam
Song writin' feels like comin' home

Chorus

Writin' Songs – on your own
Writin' songs – not alone
Writin' songs – as you roam
Writin' songs – comin' home

Maybe someday soon I'll travel free
Happy to be that guy that's me
And when I'm lonely, on my own
Writing songs will bring me home

Like finding something new at every turn
Like hearing the sound of a tumbling burn
A piece of you that's there, your own
Writing songs feels like coming home

Chorus

Chapter 3

Beyond The Mearns

Scotland's history has always been a fascination for me, the Stuart monarchy, in particular. So I decided to write two songs, one about the most tragic Mary Queen of Scots, the other about her father, the colourful James V of Scotland.

Songs
Gude Man o' Ballengeich
Mary Queen of Scots

Gude Man o' Ballengeich

This was intended as a humorous song about James V, father of Mary Queen of Scots.

Legend has it that, disguised as a beggar, he regularly visited the townfolks of Stirling.

Cramosay velvet
Slashed wi' Gold
Knit wi' horns
And lined in bold
Wi' taffeta red
The claith he liked best
And underneath a silken vest

Hamilton, Douglas
Nobles baith
Worship well
Ma' favourite claith
But in my belt's
A sharpened knife
You'd better watch yersel' at night

Chorus (jaunty vamp)
Doon the back wa'
Hoody hide
Erse hangin' oot his breeks
Mixin' wi the common folk
His name is Ballengeich

I play the lute
Wi Talie class
Maggie Erskine is
Ma' favourite lass
But Mary Guise
Ye're no tae fret
A queen is in the makin yet

O’er the ramparts
Doon back wa’
A lassie spears
Wha’s gien it awa
Why dinna ye ken
Erse oot o’ his breeks
It’s young Jamie Stewart
Auld Ballengeich

Chorus

Mary Queen of Scots

A song written to record the dreadful execution of Mary Queen of Scots; who was inhumanely axed, more than once, to prolong her agony. Her remains are still at Westminster Abbey, despite the fact that no-one wanted her in England throughout her life.

Mary Queen of Scots

Knelt on a cushion, in petticoat red
With satin and lace, last thoughts enter her head
Life pre-defined at the baptismal font
"En ma fin git mon commencement"

Papa, please help me to find a way through
In life, I have often been likened to you
You said it cam' in and would pass wi' a lass
But every turn's blocked by our Catholic mass

Mama, Mary of Guise, daughter of France
That alliance that's partnered this terrible dance
You always were there to love and protect
Be here, with me now, as I weep and reflect

In Fotheringay, ghostly loves ebb and flow
Ma Francois, Henry, James, Rizzio
So here now I kneel, blindfolded, alone
To face the blunt axe for an illusive throne

Knelt on a cushion, in petticoat red
With satin and lace, last thoughts enter her head
Life pre-defined at the baptismal font
'En ma fin git mon commencement'

(in my end be my beginning)

Chapter 4

Far Beyond the Mearns

Songs

Oh Kosovo
John Cowan

Oh Kosovo
For many Scots, it is said, 'The Rovin Dies Hard' and so it has been for me. But my reality check came during a business mission to Kosovo, soon after the country's war with Serbia. It was a check-point in my life and made me realise how fortunate I was to have lived far beyond wartime conflict and pain. I felt compelled to write about my friends there and the tragedies they had shared with me. My friends, I cry for you every time I remember what you told me. This is your song and God bless you all

The final quotation was never intended to be poetic but had to be included in the song. The song is dedicated to my friends who feature in it.

Dr. Hajredin Kucq (PhD) writes in his book 'Independence of Kosovao,' ' A major argument for the secession is based on the notion that a people which did not consent to be included in a particular state, have the moral right to decide for itself if it wants to stay within the imposed boundaries'.

Oh Kosovo

For many months I've left you, like others who have flown,
It's hard to say just how I feel – not like the life I've known,
Sometimes I feel a part of me has known you all my life,
So, what's happened to you and your ways has cut me like a knife
But one thing I am certain of, though the path be steep to climb
This land is for the people who see it all the time

The first voice said, I was a boy and with my family fled
But 20 miles from my hometown, I watched as my friends bled
The soldiers fired upon us, I saw a young child die
My friend you're not to see these things, can you hear me cry?
From refugee to poverty, that's life in Kosovo
Can I go to another life, that's what I'd like to know?
But maybe yet the mist will clear, the bell of change will chime
This land is for the people who see it all the time

The next voice said, I'd just left home, was really far too young
To be beaten up and scarred for life for talking my mother tongue
I left my kinfolk, paid my way, the borderline to cross
In England, for six years I lived, my folks to me quite lost,
When I returned to Kosovo, strangers they seemed to be,
But rather that, than join a force to fight my family,
So here I am and here I'll stay and here's my parting rhyme
This land is for the people who see it all the time

The third voice said, I had a life, a home and children five,
Three businesses I ran each day, to keep them all alive,
We fled to leave this dear land, to Canada, in fear
For 6 long years, we dreamed of home and now it's time, we're here,
But security, we have none, so we're giving it a year,
Oh how I love this land of mine but the price we pay is dear
What will you say to me, my friend? There's such a hill to climb,
This landscape's everything to me – Will I see it all the time?

The last voice was the voice of hope, putting bravely past the fears,
Giving warmth to let the poppies grow, where only once were tears
I have a hope that someday soon, we yet will see a land
Where all of us may live as one, so brother, take my hand
The bell of change has yet to chime, the wounds of Hell to heal
But there only is one hope for us, our future lives to seal
What will you say to me my friend? Is it such a hill to climb?
This land is for the people who see it all the time

(based on personal accounts shared with me by friends in Kosovo. The last verse was written on the day of the announcement of the death of Molosovitch)

John Cowan

I have many songs that I have written for my family, most of which I have decided to retain privately. However, this song was written for my grandfather who tragically lost his life in wartime conflict, far from home. I wrote a fuller account of the tragedy as a short story. This is his song , to the grandfather I never knew.

John Cowan

It's ninety years on and we've come face to face
Till now just a name, lost without trace
Your young body sunk with the SS Kutsang
A lonely day's watch as the ship's four bells rang

You sailed out in convoy from calm Plymouth Sound
Laden with arms for the Med bound
'Ease her to two revs, open half turn,
Steady to two knots and watch the ship's stern
'

Chorus
John Cowan of Arbroath a Chief Mate at Sea
No longer a medal or mystery to me
John Cowan of Arbroath a father of three
John Cowan of Arbroath, grandfather to me

In Genoa port, 'mongst wine poker and fun
Singing Loch Lomond to a red setting sun
Your Scottish voice boomed out its favourite prose
Last time you'll be heard before the day's close

O Martha, my daughters, not long now to go
Then, nearby Cape Palos, a thud felt below
A second explosion, the bright ship lights fade
The end of the Kut Sang of the China Coast Trade

Chorus

It's ninety years on and we've come face to face
I'm grandfather now in April '08
But your voice is singing your old Scottish song
John Cowan of Arbroath you'll always sing on

Printed in Great Britain
by Amazon